Books before the

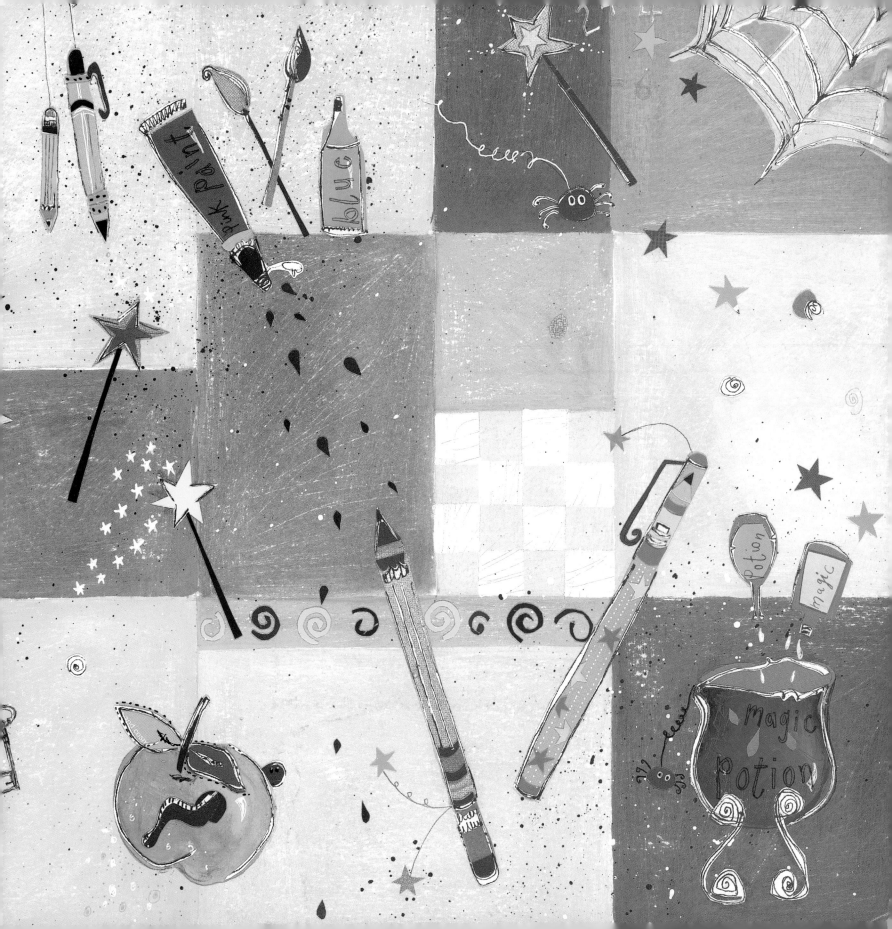

4 Mum + 4 Dad – Mark Sperring
For Mum and Dad with love –
The Pope Twins

© 2004 The Chicken House

First published in the United Kingdom in 2004 by
The Chicken House, 2 Palmer Street, Frome, Somerset, BA11 1DS
www.doublecluck.com
This edition published in 2005

Text © 2004 Mark Sperring
Illustrations © 2004 Liz and Kate Pope

Designed by Ian Butterworth

Printed and bound in Singapore

British Library Cataloguing in Publication data available
Library of Congress Cataloguing in Publication data available

ISBN: 1 904442 52 8

Wanda's First Day

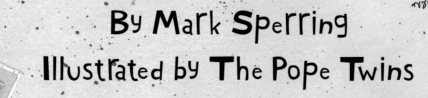

By Mark Sperring

Illustrated by The Pope Twins

The Chicken HOUSE

Wanda's mum made a lovely packed lunch for her first day at school. There were tentacle sandwiches and lizard's breath lemonade and really tasty frogspawn and rat tail yogurt.

'Remember to be wicked at school!' Wanda's mum called as she waved goodbye. 'But not *too* wicked.'

'I'll try,' Wanda promised.

As Wanda flew along she felt a little nervous. Half of her wanted to stay at home with her mum, but the other half thought it might be fun to go to school and make lots of new friends.

But when Wanda got to school and she sat at her table, she looked about and couldn't help but feel that something wasn't quite right.

'Excuse me, Miss Dewdrop,' Wanda said.

'What's wrong, dear?' her teacher asked.

Wanda whispered in Miss Dewdrop's ear, 'I don't think I'm supposed to be here. I think there's been some mistake.'

'Nonsense,' said Miss Dewdrop. 'Everyone feels a bit like that on their first day.'

Later in class, Wanda pulled her pet Frieda
from her pocket to show Tulipfluffyglow.

ribbet

ribbet

Magic

tulip

ribbet

ribbet

Story time

Secret Store

Miss Dewdrop said pets were best left at home.

At lunchtime, Wanda shared some food with Willowpeachbreath.

'These are yummy!' said Wanda, trying one of Willow's sandwiches and offering Willow one of her own.

That afternoon they all made flowers grow from seeds.

Miss Dewdrop said, 'Wanda dear, could you get your plant to put me down?'

Just before hometime, Wanda looked out of the window and saw some pupils from another school go by.

tulip's

willow's picture

by flutter

$1+3=4$

$2+1=3$

How to make Lovely flowers grow

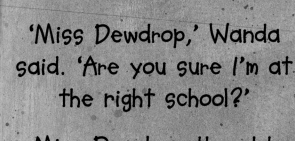

'Miss Dewdrop,' Wanda said. 'Are you sure I'm at the right school?'

Miss Dewdrop thought perhaps Wanda hadn't enjoyed herself. 'Didn't you like your first day?' she asked.

Wanda thought about the lovely food she'd eaten and the plant that she'd grown. 'Yes, I did,' Wanda said.

'And have you made some nice new friends?' Miss Dewdrop asked.

Wanda thought about Tulipfluffyglow and Willowpeachbreath. 'I suppose I have!' Wanda said, smiling.

magic

'Then don't you like your teacher?' Miss Dewdrop asked.
Wanda blushed and said she thought Miss Dewdrop was lovely.
'Well then,' said Miss Dewdrop, 'you're definitely at the right school
and we shall all look forward to seeing you tomorrow.'

School be

School
hometime

fairy flowers

That night, snuggled up in bed, Wanda decided that the next day she would take something

extra nice and extra lovely for Miss Dewdrop . . . .

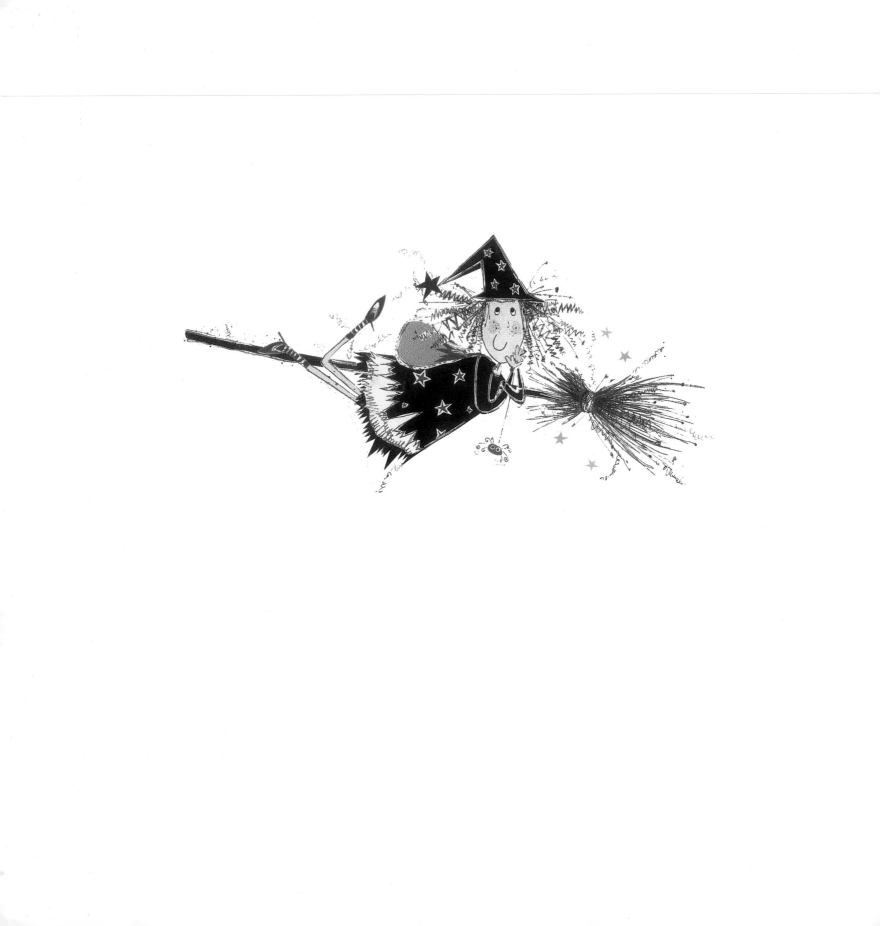